TONY BRA

ATTACK
OF THE
VIKINGS

BLOOMSBURY EDUCATION
AN IMPRINT OF BLOOMSBURY
LONDON OXFORD NEW YORK NEW DELHI SYDNEY

Bloomsbury Education
An imprint of Bloomsbury Publishing Plc

50 Bedford Square
London
WC1B 3DP
UK

1385 Broadway
New York
NY 10018
USA

www.bloomsbury.com

BLOOMSBURY and the Diana logo are trademarks of Bloomsbury Publishing Plc

First published in 2017 by Bloomsbury Education

ISBN
PB: 978-1-4729-2940-2
ePub: 978-1-4729-2941-9
ePDF: 978-1-4729-2942-6

2 4 6 8 10 9 7 5 3 1

Typeset by Newgen Knowledge Works (P), Chennai, India
Printed and bound in the UK by CPI Group (UK) Ltd, Croydon CR0 4YY

To find out more about our authors and books visit www.bloomsbury.com. Here you will
find extracts, author interviews, details of forthcoming events and the option
to sign up for our newsletters.

This one is for Henry Treece – and Akira Kurosawa

Cry havoc, and let slip the dogs of war!
                              – William Shakespeare

CONTENTS

CHAPTER ONE

A Loud Voice

T he red autumn sun was hanging low in the sky when Finn and his friends Egil and Njal returned to the village. They had spent most of the day in the forest, but the growling of their stomachs had finally brought them back. Egil and Njal were looking forward to their evening meal, and chattered cheerfully. Finn however was quiet, his mood darkening with each pace that took him closer to home.

'Cheer up, Finn,' said Egil as they passed through the gate of the stockade. As usual, the platform that ran inside it was empty of guards. 'Why are you miserable, anyway? I wish I was going on the voyage to the Southern Isles.'

'Fine, I'll ask my father if you can go instead of me,' said Finn. 'I went last year and I told you, there's nothing more boring. It's a lot of sailing around from island to island, talking to other farmers and trying to persuade them to trade with us.'

'Well, I think it sounds like fun,' said Njal. 'At least you get to visit somewhere different and meet new people. Nothing ever happens here.'

Njal was right about that, Finn thought. Behind them the village's sheep, a jostling flock of bleating woolly-backs, were being herded in for the night from beyond the wall. The shepherds were a couple of very young boys, but the real work was being done by two sheepdogs that snapped at the flock like wolves. It was all too familiar, the kind of thing Finn had seen every day of his life.

He had known Egil and Njal his whole life as well. The three of them were about the same age, fourteen summers or so, and they had always been friends. Egil was short and dark and full of jokes and mischief, while Njal was pale and good-natured and had a nest of flame-coloured hair sitting on top of his bony head. Finn's hair was light brown, and he was taller than Egil, but shorter than Njal. They wore the same kind of clothes – dun-coloured tunics, baggy leggings, and leather ankle boots.

'My father's going to be cross that I wasn't here to help load the ships today,' said Finn. They had come to an open space a spear's throw from the forest gate, the point where their paths went different ways.

'Will he beat you?' said Njal, his voice full of concern.

'I don't think so,' said Finn. 'He'll just do a lot of shouting.'

'So what in Thor's name are you worried about?' said Egil. 'A bit of yelling won't hurt you – words aren't swords. I take no notice when my father shouts at me.'

'His voice isn't as loud as my father's,' said Finn. But then Finn's father, Ottar, was chief of the village, and it was useful for the most important man to have the loudest voice. Ottar sorted out arguments and disputes, and called meetings if he needed to make an announcement or explain a difficult decision. The villagers generally trusted his judgement, though usually he had to yell so they could hear him.

'Maybe we should come with you,' said Njal.

'Don't worry, I'll be fine,' said Finn. 'I'll stay out of his way.'

'Fair enough,' said Egil. Then he gave Finn a wicked smile. 'And of course, if it does go badly, we'll make sure you get a wonderful funeral, like a proper Viking.'

'Very funny,' said Finn. 'See you both tomorrow... I hope!'

They separated and headed for their homes. Finn's path to his father's hall took him through the main part of the village, up a muddy street of log-walled houses. The settlement wasn't large. Just fifty Norse families lived there, the houses clustered round a small bay on the coast of Alba, on land seized by Finn's great-grandfather from the Gaelic-speaking tribe who had lived there originally. To the west of the village was the cold vastness of the Great Ocean. To the east, beyond the fields they planted with crops, was a dark, dense forest and behind that were the mountains, their high rocky peaks capped with snow. The Orkney Isles lay three days' sailing to the north, and the Southern Isles were the same distance in the opposite direction.

The sun was finally sinking into the sea, and lamps were being lit – warm yellow pools of light spilling from doorways where mothers called to their children. Finn trudged past, the chill air full of the tang of woodsmoke from the evening cooking fires. At last he came to his father's hall. It stood on a rise in the heart of the village and was the biggest house by far. The walls were made of sturdy pine logs, and the main beam of its turf roof was curved like the spine of a great whale. Two huge crossed beams framed the front like the horns of some legendary beast, and the doorposts were covered in carvings of heroes and gods to ward off evil. Above the doors was the face of Odin the All-Father, the one-eyed god who ruled the world.

Finn stopped and looked at him. 'Great Odin,' he murmured under his breath, 'why have the Fates given me this life when I want another?' He hated the thought of being a farmer, though he felt he was doomed to end up that way, just like his father. Everyone seemed to expect it of him in any case. But there was another future path he dreamed of, one that would surely lead to adventure and glory, wealth and fame. Finn wanted to be a Viking, a mighty lord of war, leading his warriors into the storm of battle.

He had heard of such men in tales told by the villagers around his father's hearth on winter evenings, and often imagined himself into their stories. They were great heroes who defeated hordes of enemies, and they always died holding a sword so that Odin would send his shield maidens, the Valkyries, to take them to Valhalla, the great hall of warriors in Asgard, where the gods lived.

Now Finn could see himself standing proudly at the prow of his own longship, his silver chain mail and helmet shining, his hand gripping the hilt of a fine sword. He would give it a name, of course, something terrifying like Neck-Biter or Dragon-Fang. The sun would flash off its steel blade as he drew it, and his enemies would fall before him.

A piglet squealed and ran past, with a small girl chasing after it, splashing his legs with mud. Finn snapped back into the moment and sighed. Odin's face was unchanged, so it seemed the god would give him no answer today. He took a deep breath, let it out slowly, pushed open the hall doors, and slipped inside. There was a chance his father might still be out somewhere – the village chief was always busy.

The hall was full of noise and movement, the usual early evening hustle and bustle. A couple of servants were lighting the oil lamps that hung on the walls, while two more tended the large cooking pot that hung over the hearth-fire, its fragrant steam rising to the smoke-hole in the roof. Finn's stepmother Astrid was giving orders to yet another servant, and his stepsister Gunnhild was sitting on a bench behind her.

Astrid's gown was blue with an embroidered hem of silver thread, and Gunnhild's was red. Mother and daughter were both small and slight, and both had hair the colour of summer wheat. Finn had few memories of his own mother, who had died of the coughing sickness when he was five. His father had remarried three years ago – Astrid was a widow – and at first Finn had been worried that he and his stepmother would argue, something he had seen in other families. But luckily they liked each other, and got on well.

It was a different matter with Gunnhild, though. She and Finn had never hit it off, and they bickered a lot. Astrid thought it was because of the gap in their ages – Gunnhild was only twelve. But Finn had a feeling it was because Gunnhild knew he had no time for girls, and she resented that. She stuck her tongue out at him now, and as usual he did his best to ignore her.

'Ah, the wanderer returns,' boomed a loud voice. 'And where have you been?'

Finn froze as his father emerged from the shadows at the far end of the hall. He stood staring at Finn across the burning logs inside the wide ring of large, flat stones that made up the hall's central hearth. Ottar was a big man, with broad shoulders and hands the size of shovel blades. His thick, dark hair and beard were touched with grey, and his eyes were the green of northern seas. He was wearing his working clothes, a rough old tunic and trousers that Astrid often threatened to burn.

'I'm sorry, Father,' said Finn. 'I... I meant to come home sooner, but...'

'Spare me the excuses, Finn,' said Ottar, shaking his head. Everyone else in the hall stopped what they were doing to watch and listen. From the corner of his eye Finn could see Gunnhild smirking. 'We both know the truth,' Finn's father continued. 'You don't want to come on the trading voyage because you think it's boring, unlike the dreams of being a Viking hero your head is full of, and you've been doing whatever you can to get out of coming with me. That's right, is it not?'

Finn stared back at him for the space of half a dozen heartbeats, and their eyes locked together. 'I can't help the way I feel, Father,' he said, shrugging.

Ottar sighed, and shook his head. 'Still, at least you're honest, so maybe I haven't done too badly in bringing you up,' he said, but then he paused. Finn could see he was turning something over in his mind. 'Very well,' the chief said at last. 'I will relieve you of your burden, Finn, even though most sons would think it a great honour to go on such a voyage with their father. This time you can stay at home in the village – but there is one condition. You will take my place while I am away.'

At first Finn couldn't quite believe what he had just heard, and he frowned. Then it sank in, and his heart lifted. 'I swear I won't let you down, Father,' he said.

He smiled for the first time that day, excited at the prospect of doing something different, something that would help him prove himself worthy to his father.

What could possibly go wrong?

CHAPTER TWO

Real Weapons

Finn's father called a meeting the next morning, and everyone crowded into his hall. The chief came straight to the point, and told the villagers he would be leaving his son in charge while he was away.

Some of the men glanced at each other.

'Are you sure about that, Ottar?' said Kalf, a grumpy older fellow. Kalf had an ugly face and a bushy tuft of white hair that stuck up on top of his bald head, and he never missed a chance to criticise or sneer at others. His nickname in the village was Kalf the Sour. 'The boy is far too young to take on such a responsibility.'

There were some mutterings of agreement from the people around Kalf. Finn was standing at his father's right hand and felt his cheeks beginning to turn red.

'Yes, I am sure,' growled Ottar, glaring at Kalf. 'I was much the same age as Finn when my own father died and left me to care for my mother. Besides, how will he learn to be a man unless he does the things men have to do?'

Finn glanced at his father. He had known that Ingvar, his grandfather, had died when Ottar was young. But Finn hadn't realised quite how young he had been. Well, like father, like son, Finn told himself, proud that he was being given this chance to be in charge, and convinced he would rise to the challenge. He glimpsed Njal and Egil in the crowd, they were both grinning at him, and he grinned back. Then he saw Gunnhild. She was looking at him with a raised eyebrow and the same smirk as before.

'Well, if you put it that way...' Kalf was muttering, clearly irritated.

'I do,' said Ottar. 'Anyone else got something to say?' He surveyed the crowd and waited for a moment, but nobody spoke. 'Right, that's settled,' he said. 'Finn will be in charge, and if you have a problem, you go to him as you would to me.'

The rest of the day passed in continued preparations for the voyage. The village had two ships – not lean, beautiful, deadly Viking longships with dragon prows, but stubby knarrs that were slow and steady and could take plenty of cargo. This time Finn did his share of work with the other boys and men, loading the ships with baskets of vegetables, barrels of their own ale, and bales of homespun wool.

'We'll be gone ten days, maybe a little longer,' said Finn's father when the loading was finished. They were standing on the quayside, looking down at the two ships below. The sun was sinking into the sea in a blaze of fire, the shadows deepening, and a cold wind was whipping in from the mountains. 'If you're not sure what to do, ask Astrid. Your stepmother has plenty of common sense. That's why I married her.'

'Yes, Father,' said Finn, and waited for more advice. But none came.

The ships left at dawn the next day, on the ebb tide, their crews rowing clear of the bay before raising the sails and turning southwards. In them went all the young and fit men of the village, leaving only the old and the women, the boys and girls.

Finn watched the ships from the quayside until he could see them no more.

* * *

Nothing much happened for the rest of that day, or the next. Finn kept himself in readiness, waiting for someone to come to him with a problem or a dispute. But life in the village continued calmly, everybody just getting on with normal things.

'This isn't very exciting, is it?' said Egil. 'I was hoping we'd be busier.'

It was a fine autumn day, the air was cool, the sun high in a clear blue sky. Finn was sitting with Egil and Njal on the guest bench outside his father's hall. He had told his friends they could be the first two warriors in his war-band, and Egil had instantly claimed the right to be his second in command. Njal had simply smiled and shrugged, but Finn had said they were both his shield-brothers, and equal in his eyes.

'We should be glad it's quiet,' Njal said. 'We don't want any trouble.'

Finn wasn't so sure. How could he prove to his father he knew what it was to be a man if he didn't actually *do* anything while he was away? He needed at least a few achievements to report on... Suddenly he had an idea, and jumped to his feet.

'Come on, let's take a walk around the village,' he said eagerly. 'My father always does that when he has a spare moment, just to check all is well.'

'Like guards doing their rounds in a fort...' murmured Egil. 'But we should do it properly. Warriors don't go on patrol without weapons, do they?'

'You're right,' said Finn, nodding. 'We'd better see what we can find.'

Finn led his friends into the hall. He thought his father and the other men had probably taken most of the village's real weapons with them – the long knives that could pass for swords, the best hunting spears – a wise precaution on any voyage. But there was a large storeroom at the rear of the hall, and Finn was hoping they might have left something behind. The third chest they opened revealed a surprise.

Egil pulled out an iron helmet, a short mail-shirt and a sword in a plain wooden scabbard, complete with belt. The helmet was badly dented, the mail-shirt was ragged, the sword was battered and blunt, and they were all covered in spots of rust.

'I wonder who they belong to,' said Njal. 'Are they your father's, Finn?'

'I doubt it,' said Finn, feeling puzzled. He had never seen them before, and he couldn't believe they were anything to do with his father. Ottar Ingvarsson was a farmer, not a fighter. 'I suppose they might have been my grandfather's...'

'It doesn't really matter, does it?' laughed Egil. 'They belong to us now!'

Finn laughed as well, and as chief in his father's stead, he quickly claimed the sword. Egil chose the helmet, even though it was a little too big for him, which left the mail-shirt for Njal. 'Good, we're ready,' said Finn. 'Follow me, men!'

They set out on their patrol of the village, Finn proudly leading the way. They did a full circuit – down the main street, along to the stretch where the wall of the stockade faced the quayside, then back up to the gate and down to the beach on the far side. They passed quite a few people, most of whom paid them no attention, although Kalf made sure to give them a sour look. At one point a gaggle of younger children started following, but Finn quickly chased them off.

After a while they headed back to the hall. The three of them were laughing, enjoying themselves, but then they bumped into Gunnhild. She was with two dark-haired girls, her friends Freydis and Signy. They were both taller than Gunnhild, yet Finn knew they thought of his stepsister as their leader. Finn went to step round them, but Gunnhild blocked his path, staring at him with her infuriating smirk.

'Where in Freya's name did you get that ancient sword?' she said. 'It makes you look even more ridiculous than usual. And as for your daft friends...'

'Why don't you just run along, Gunnhild?' said Finn, determined to give as good as he got. 'Shouldn't you be sewing, or spinning, or whatever it is girls do?'

'So speaks the hero,' said Gunnhild, 'the boy who is going to protect us while the real men are away. If you ask me, Ottar should have left my mother in charge.'

'Nobody *is* asking you,' said Finn, pushing past. 'And my father chose *me*.'

'Well, let me know if you need any help,' said Gunnhild. 'We'd hate to see you make a mess of things, wouldn't we, girls? You'd never live it down.'

Gunnhild and her friends burst out laughing. Finn scowled at her and stomped off, with Egil and Njal hurrying after him. The three of them finally reached the hall, where they sat on the guest bench in the sunlight, muttering and complaining about girls. They kept telling each other all the clever answers they should have given Gunnhild, and then Egil walked up and down pretending to be a girl and mimicking the way she had spoken. It wasn't long before the three friends were laughing once more.

'Anyway, we can relax now,' said Finn. 'We've done our work for the day.'

'What about Ylva and Kjartan?' said Njal. 'Shouldn't we check on them too?'

Ylva was the wise woman people went to for potions and herbs to cure their sicknesses, and salves for their wounds. She was part of the village, but chose to live outside the stockade, in a hut at the edge of the forest. She was tiny and white-haired, always wore a long black gown, and seemed incredibly old. Some people thought she was scary, perhaps a witch, but Astrid scoffed at that and said Ylva had a kind heart.

Kjartan was old too. He had turned up at the village a few years ago, and Finn's father had given him shelter for a while. But eventually he chose to live outside as well, in a hut near Ylva's. He was tall, and his long hair was mostly grey. He kept himself to himself, rarely spoke, and never came into the village. There had been a time when people wondered what his story was, but now nobody really gave it much thought.

'No, I'm sure they're all right,' said Finn. 'We can visit them tomorrow.'

He realised that Njal was no longer listening to him, however. Both of Finn's friends were looking upwards with puzzled frowns on their faces, and Finn turned to see what had caught their attention. A distant column of black smoke was rising high into the cloudless blue sky, somewhere to the north of the village.

'I don't like the look of that,' said Egil. Finn didn't like the look of it either.

He only hoped it didn't mean trouble.

But it did.

CHAPTER THREE
Fire and Sword

Others had seen the column of smoke, and a murmuring crowd soon gathered in the open space outside the hall, the place in the village with the best view north. Most of them thought a fire in the forest must be the cause.

'Don't be stupid,' said Kalf. 'Smoke from a forest fire never rises straight up like that! Besides, any fool knows that the forest is too damp in the autumn for a fire.'

'Well, as you're so clever, perhaps you can tell us what is going on,' said Egil.

'I most certainly can, boy,' snapped Kalf. 'That's the kind of smoke you get when houses burn. And I'd be willing to wager it's coming from Andari's village.'

Finn felt worry touch his heart. Andari was chief of the next settlement up the coast, and a good friend of his father's. Many of Ottar's people had friends in Andari's village, and a few even had kin there. Fire was a constant danger in villages like theirs, where the houses were built of wood and had roofs of thatch or turf.

'Shouldn't we do something?' Finn said. 'We ought to go and help.'

'There's no point,' said Kalf. 'It would take a day at least to walk that far through the forest. So whatever is happening will be over long before you arrive.'

Finn knew Kalf was right. He would just have to wait for his father to come home, and in the meantime pray to Odin that Andari and the people of his village were unharmed. But he was left feeling unsatisfied and powerless, and he wondered if everyone was looking at him and wishing his father hadn't left him in charge. The crowd eventually broke up, but Finn watched the smoke for the rest of that day.

He rose early the next morning and went outside to gaze north. The sky was grey with clouds and the column of smoke had disappeared, leaving only a faint haze beyond the forest. Finn turned to go back into the hall, but then he saw Egil running towards him, the expression on his face a mixture of shock and excitement.

'You must come to the quayside, Finn!' he said, panting. 'Quickly!'

'Why? What's going on?' Finn asked. But Egil had dashed off again, down towards the harbour, without answering. Finn frowned and followed, hurrying past quiet houses where families still slept, and others where they were beginning to wake and think about making the morning meal as the village stirred to face the new day.

Egil was waiting at the quayside, along with Njal and Kalf and several more villagers. Everyone was looking at something down below. Finn pushed through and saw it was a small, one-masted sailing boat crammed full of people. There were three men and half a dozen women, most clutching tiny babies or children. One of the men was wounded, his head swathed in bloodstained rags, and they all looked worn out and frightened. The children were deathly pale, their faces stained with tears.

'Well, don't just stand there!' said Finn at once. 'Help them ashore!'

It took a while to get all the people off the boat and on to the quayside, but they managed it at last. Finn recognised one of the women. Her name was Solveig, and she was Andari's wife. She had two small children with her, a boy and a girl.

'Don't worry, you are safe now,' said Finn. 'What happened?'

'The sea-wolves came with fire and sword,' said Solveig, her voice trembling. 'They burned our village and killed everyone who tried to stand against them.'

'What about your husband?' said Finn, his heart sinking. 'He is not with you.'

'We were the only ones to escape,' she said. 'Andari got us to the boat, and then...'

She could say no more and broke down, crying and pulling her children close. They sobbed too. Finn wished he could comfort them, but he knew words wouldn't help. 'Sea-wolves' was another name for pirates, raiders who took the whale's road and attacked villages for plunder and slaves, who looted and burned and killed. There had been no reports of such raids on this coast for a long time.

Now it seemed the sea-wolves had returned.

*   *   *

Finn and the others helped the survivors from Andari's village up to the hall, where Astrid immediately set about caring for them. She ordered the servants to bring dry clothes, and made sure they had something to eat, especially the children. Ylva appeared, seemingly without being summoned by anyone, and tended to the wounded man, salving the cuts on his head and binding them with clean linen.

The news flew quickly round the settlement, and before long a noisy crowd of inquisitive villagers had gathered outside the hall. The boldest among them pushed open the doors so they could gawp at the survivors and call out questions.

'Be off with you!' Astrid said, shooing them away. 'These poor people are in no state to talk to anyone. Finn will call a meeting later to tell you more – won't you, Finn?'

'What?' said Finn, surprised, and Astrid gave him a look. 'Er... yes, of course,' he said. 'We will have a village meeting here later, after the midday meal.'

It was clearly the right thing to do – the villagers deserved to know what was going on. Even so, Finn felt cross with himself. He should have known what to do without being told by his stepmother – his father wouldn't have needed that. Finn saw Gunnhild shaking her head in disbelief, and he walked away, his cheeks hot.

The morning turned cold and wet, with a sharp wind from the sea bringing rain, and people began to gather in the hall as soon as the midday meal was finished. The servants set out benches and Astrid took a place at the front, as befitted the lady of the house, with Gunnhild next to her. The survivors from Andari's village sat on one side of the hearth, Solveig and her children in the middle of them. Finn stood on the other side, flanked by Egil and Njal, and waited until everyone fell silent. He felt strange, as if he was pretending to be his father, but he had thought about what to say.

'Welcome to the hall of my father, and his father before him,' he said, changing the usual words of the chief's greeting. 'We are gathered to hear what has happened to our friends, the people of Andari's village. Can you tell us now, Solveig?'

'I... I can,' Solveig said. 'They came at night, when we were sleeping...'

She spoke quietly, the sound of the rain almost drowning out her voice. It seemed that men from a longship had landed and forced their way through the gates of the village's stockade, which had been unguarded. They had set houses alight with torches and killed people as they ran out, although they had allowed some to live – the ones they wanted to sell as slaves. The men had tried to fight back, but they hadn't stood a chance against warriors armed with swords and spears and axes.

As soon as she had finished speaking, a few of those sitting on the benches called out, asking if their kin and friends might also have escaped in some way. Solveig said nothing, but shook her head at each name, and screams soon filled the hall.

'Who are these sea-wolves?' said Finn at last. 'Where are they from?'

'Only the gods can tell you that,' said Solveig. 'They speak Norse, the same tongue as us, but they are too cruel to be ordinary men. Their chief strode among them like a creature of darkness. He has raven-black hair with a streak of pure white in it and a scar running over one eye, and he laughed as he killed Andari...'

'Oh, don't worry, he's a man all right,' said a voice. 'His name is Red Swein.'

Finn looked round and saw that it was Ylva who had spoken. She was sitting beside Astrid, and everyone else in the hall was now staring at her in surprise.

'So, you've heard of this man,' said Finn. 'What can you tell us about him?'

'There's only one thing you need to know,' said Kalf. He was sitting behind Ylva, but now he stood up to address the hall. 'Sea-wolves don't just raid a single village and then disappear. They always attack as many as they can in one voyage.'

'What are you saying?' a man murmured. 'You think they'll come here?'

'Oh yes,' said Kalf. 'In fact I'm as sure of it as I'm certain the sun will rise tomorrow. They will come, and they will do the same to us. Our only chance is to flee, to run deep into the forest and hide until they have gone away...'

There were loud groans and cries of alarm, and then the villagers started to yell and talk over each other, most of them agreeing with Kalf. Finn looked on, bewildered, wondering just how the old man had managed to take over the meeting so easily. Then he felt a sudden wave of anger, and he knew he had to regain control or lose it forever. And there was only one way to do that – his father's way.

'SILENCE!' Finn yelled at the top of his voice, his words ringing around the hall. Everyone stopped talking, and all eyes turned to him. 'We will not flee into the forest. We will stay in our village, and if the sea-wolves come – well, then we will fight them.'

Finn had never felt anything so strongly before in his life. It was as if Odin himself had whispered in his ear: *this will be your chance to show your father that you can be a great warrior*. What fame he would win if these sea-wolves came to the village and he led his people in defeating them! Songs would be sung about such a hero until the day of Ragnarok, when the world was doomed to end in blood and fire.

This was his moment, and he would seize it with all his might.

CHAPTER FOUR
Thunder Rumbling

It didn't end there, of course – after Finn had spoken, the yelling started once more, and then went on for a long time. Kalf kept shouting the same thing again and again – they should flee into the forest as soon as possible – and plenty of people agreed. Then Finn said they would only have to hold out for a few days, just until his father and the other men returned, which swayed many over to his side.

'Don't listen to the boy!' Kalf yelled, so cross his eyes were almost popping out of his skull.

'Ottar would agree with me. He always listens to my advice!'

'He does not,' said Astrid with a snort of derision. 'You're the last person my husband would take advice from, and Finn knows his father's mind better than you do. Ottar left Finn in charge, and Finn has spoken. There is nothing more to say.'

Finn nodded. 'The meeting is over,' he said. 'Go back to your homes.'

'But what happens now?' said a woman. 'What do you want us to do?'

Good question, thought Finn, wishing he had an answer for her. But he didn't. 'Er... no need to worry about that now,' he said. 'I will tell you all later.'

There was some grumbling, and Finn could see Kalf wanted to keep the argument going. The old man couldn't stand up to Astrid's icy gaze, though. He turned on his heel and left the hall muttering, and everyone else trailed out behind him.

'We should talk, Finn,' said Astrid, and walked off towards the chamber she shared with Finn's father. Finn told Egil and Njal he would see them later, and followed after her.

The chamber was at the rear of the hall. A large wooden bed covered in furs stood against one wall, its headboard filled with a carving of the goddess Freya, her eyes like stars and the lines of her long hair merging into the waves of the sea. Astrid was sitting on a low settle by another wall, and Finn sat down beside her.

'Thank you, Astrid,' he said. 'I thought he was never going to shut up.'

Astrid smiled. 'We had all heard more than enough from Kalf the Sour for one day. And I meant what I said. You know your father's mind much better than Kalf does.'

'So, you think my father would agree with me? He would stay and fight?'

'Yes, I am sure he would. We have all worked so hard over many years to make this village what it is today, and your father would not want to see it destroyed by these sea-wolves. Besides, we cannot flee into the forest in this weather.'

Finn hadn't thought of that. It was still raining, the wind was moaning and gusting and rattling the doors of the hall like a great beast scrabbling to get in, and thunder rumbled over the mountains as if Thor was beating them with his giant hammer. The village always lost a few of the weak and the old when the weather turned bad in the autumn and winter, usually from the coughing sickness that had killed Finn's mother. How many more would die if they spent days in the forest without any shelter?

'The only trouble is... I don't exactly know how we *can* fight,' Finn said. It was good to hear Astrid thought his father would approve of what he was doing, but that didn't make it any easier. The truth was that the feeling he'd had in front of everyone in the hall had faded. Now his stomach was beginning to churn with worries – how could they hope to resist armed warriors? What should they actually *do*? Why had he opened his mouth and said such a stupid thing? Maybe Kalf was right after all...

'We have the stockade,' said Astrid, shrugging. 'It will be hard for anybody to climb over if we guard it – we must have enough people for that. You should try to get Kalf on your side, though. Men like him need to feel important, and he'll keep telling everyone you're a fool until he does. So, find him something to do.'

They talked for what seemed like a long time, Astrid making other suggestions, and Finn felt his confidence return. Perhaps it *would* be possible, he thought, the outline of a plan beginning to form in his mind. He just had to keep his nerve, like the heroes in the stories and songs. In fact, he thought to himself with a smile, his fame and glory would be even greater because the odds against him were so high...

'One last thing, Finn,' said Astrid, taking his hand. 'Your father thought leaving you in charge while he was away would be good for you, perhaps help you to see what really matters in life and grow up a little. He certainly didn't think anything like this would happen. You have a much harder test to face than he ever imagined, but don't be downhearted. I am sure you will get through it.'

Finn thanked her again, pleased that at least one person believed in him.

* * *

He had worked out his plan by the time he caught up with Egil and Njal. 'It's simple,' he said as he led his friends back to the hall. The wind and rain had eased, but the sky was filled with grey clouds, and great rags of white mist hung around the mountain peaks. 'We make the village a fortress – we allow nobody to enter or leave. We bring in the flocks and herds, we close the gates and seal them, we man the walls.'

'What, just us three?' said Egil, scowling. 'That's not going to work, is it?'

'No, you idiot,' said Finn. 'We'll need as many people as we can get. I want you to round up all the boys who are more than ten summers old. Njal, you're to collect weapons – axes, hunting spears, knives, things that could be made into clubs. Take whatever you can find and bring it here to the hall. Is that understood?'

They both grinned and nodded, then ran in different directions to do his bidding.

Finn, meanwhile, went off to talk to Kalf. The old man lived with his wife in a small house at the other end of the village. Kalf kept a couple of pigs in his front yard, and had a chicken coop at the side. Finn knocked on his door and Kalf opened it.

'What do you want, boy?' he snarled. 'We have nothing to say to each other.'

'Listen, Kalf, I'm sorry we quarrelled, and I hope we can put it behind us. But that's not the only reason I'm here. I've come to ask for your help. I need a man with lots of experience, a man that everybody in the village has learned to respect.'

'Your stepmother didn't pay me much respect earlier,' Kalf muttered.

'You're right, and I'm sorry about that too,' said Finn. 'I hope you can forgive her. I know my father thinks very highly of you, whatever Astrid might say...'

Finn kept talking, piling on the praise and flattery, and Kalf lapped it all up. Finally Finn asked the old man for a special favour, saying that only Kalf could do it.

'So, you want *me* to ask the older men to guard the walls alongside the boys?' said Kalf. 'You're right, of course, I *am* the best man to take on that task. I'm still thinking of leaving, you know. But I suppose I could help you get organised before I go.'

Finn walked away, pleased the trick had worked, yet hardly able to believe it had been so easy. He had learned a lesson about people – thanks to Astrid.

Later that day he stood at the door of his father's hall with Egil and Njal on one side and Kalf on the other, watching the village's boys and older men assemble in front of them. There were fifty or so, the youngest a boy who didn't know if he was nine or ten summers, the oldest a grey-beard who said he was sixty. But he had lost most of his memory as well as most of his teeth, so he could have been much older. The rest were boys younger than Finn, and men older than his father – or even Kalf.

'Look at them,' Egil murmured. 'They won't make much of a war-band.'

Finn's heart sank – he could see what Egil meant. Many of the boys were small and skinny, and the men were all shapes and sizes. Quite a few had big bellies, or were stooped over from years of back-breaking farm work in the fields and sheepfolds. He knew some of them were still strong, and most knew how to use an axe to cut down a tree, or a spear on a hunting trip. But apart from the occasional brawl when they had drunk too much ale, none had any experience of fighting.

'We don't have to be a proper war-band,' said Njal. 'We won't be fighting the sea-wolves in the open, will we? We just need to keep them out of the village.'

'Quite right,' said Kalf. 'And we older men can manage that by ourselves. You young pups will probably get in our way, so it's best if you leave it to us.'

Egil rolled his eyes, which made Kalf angry, and they started arguing. Njal tried to make peace between them, but it was Finn who finally made them stop.

'That's enough!' he said. 'No more arguing! We are all in this together!'

'Is that so?' said a voice behind him. 'You seem to have left us girls out.'

Finn turned round and saw it was Gunnhild. She had come out of the hall with Freydis and Signy. The three of them stood facing him, their arms crossed.

'Don't be stupid, Gunnhild,' he said. 'You girls have no part to play in this.'

Gunnhild opened her mouth as if she wanted to say something else. But she thought better of it, glared at him instead, and stomped back into the hall, followed by her friends. Now it was Finn's turn to roll his eyes, and the three boys laughed.

Then Finn glanced at the sky and frowned. The red sun was low in the far west, the undersides of the clouds over the sea glowing with fire from its dying rays. There was still much to do before night fell, when the sea-wolves might come.

Finn's stomach clenched – what if they were already on their way?

CHAPTER FIVE

Out of the Darkness

It took a while to get things organised to Finn's satisfaction. Njal had collected plenty of weapons, including some hunting bows, and he and Egil handed them out, something that caused bickering about who should have what. Then Finn divided everybody into two groups, one to man the walls by day, the other by night, although this led to more grumbling and lots of men wanting to swap for no good reason.

Some of the village's women turned up as well, mothers who had come to reclaim their sons because they thought them too young to be involved, and wives who thought their husbands were too old. Several men and boys tried to resist, and Finn backed them up, saying he needed them all. But the women would have none of it, and dragged off men and boys alike. Finn soon realised he'd lost a dozen of his war-band.

At dusk, the flocks and herds were brought into the village animal pens as usual. The gates facing the forest were closed and sealed with a thick beam across the inside, and Finn ordered the night guards to take up position on the stockade. They climbed the ladders to the platform, but it was soon clear there weren't enough of them to make sure they would be evenly spaced around the entire village.

'So let's not have two separate groups of guards, then,' said Egil, shrugging. 'We should just put everyone on the walls and keep them there the whole time.'

'No, that way we would get too tired, especially if we have to stand watch for two or three days and nights,' said Finn. 'And remember, Solveig said the raiders who attacked Andari's village came from the sea – they're called sea-wolves, after all. I think we should put most of the guards on the stockade where it faces the Great Ocean. We'll only need a few guards over on the forest side, just to be safe.'

Night was falling, blackness spreading swiftly across the sky. Finn, Egil and Njal climbed up to the platform above the gate that gave access to the quayside and the beach. Behind them the village lay hushed, as if all the houses seemed to be holding their breath. Yellow lamplight spilled from their doors, and curls of smoke from the evening cooking fires caught the silver glow of the rising half-moon. Torches stood at intervals around the stockade, their leaping red flames like splashes of blood against the dark. A dog barked, and a baby was crying.

'We forgot about Ylva and Kjartan again,' said Njal. 'They're still outside.'

Finn felt a pang of guilt. 'There's nothing we can do about it now,' he said. 'They should be safe where they are. Or we'll just have to hope they will be, anyway.'

Egil and Njal went off round the stockade to check on the guards, leaving Finn by himself. He tried not to think about the two old people in the forest, and concentrated on what was in front of him. The sea gleamed beneath the light of the half-moon, with small waves whispering every so often on the soft sand of the beach and gently slapping against the timbers of the quayside. Finn leaned on the top of the stockade and stared into the distance, straining his eyes to search for the sail of a longship. But he could see nothing, just the sea merging into thick blackness where it met the sky.

There was no wind, yet it was cold, and Finn was glad Astrid had made him wear his warm winter cloak. He pulled it more tightly around him, and a fold snagged on the hilt of his sword, the one he had found in the hall's storeroom. Now he found himself wondering if he would be able to use it should the sea-wolves attack. He peered over the stockade, which was almost the height of two men on this side of the village, and imagined a sea-wolf climbing up towards him. What would it be like to strike out with the sword, to feel it clanging on a helmet – or slicing into a man's flesh?

Finn gripped the hilt and gritted his teeth. He wanted to be a Viking, didn't he? So, he would do whatever it took to protect his village and his people. Anyway, he was sure proper fighting couldn't be that hard. It certainly sounded easy in all the stories and songs he had heard, as men did what came naturally, even taking pleasure in killing their enemies. He imagined himself into his favourite tales of great heroes.

Then he realised he was shivering, and it wasn't because of the cold.

* * *

It was the shouting that woke him. At first it was part of his dream, the voices of the warriors he was fighting in his sleep, but soon his eyes flickered open and he fell out of the dream world and back into the real one. Finn had been tired, and had rested his head on the top of the stockade, and he had no idea how much time had passed. Now he scanned the sea, his heart pounding so hard it seemed to have leaped into his throat. Yet he could see no longship at anchor – the noise was coming from elsewhere.

Suddenly Egil and Njal appeared beside him out of the darkness. 'Something is happening at the forest gate, Finn!' Egil said breathlessly. 'What shall we do?'

Finn quickly pulled himself together and looked in that direction. Shadows were moving on the stockade, and several people seemed to be holding torches aloft. There was shouting, but it was impossible to tell what was being said.

'You two, come with me!' Finn said, scrambling down the nearest ladder. 'Everyone else, stay in your positions. It could be a trick!'

He ran through the village, with Egil and Njal close behind. People appeared in doorways, their faces pale with fear, and some called out, but Finn didn't answer. He came at last to the forest gate and looked up at the platform above it. The guards he had left there – Kalf, another older man called Ranulf, and Bjarni, a twelve-year-old boy – were each holding a torch, and Kalf was shouting at somebody outside.

'Open up, I say!' a rough voice replied from beyond the gate, and then there was pounding on it hard enough to rattle the timbers and shake the cross-beam.

'What's going on, Kalf?' Finn shouted up at the old man. 'Who is it?'

'Who do you think it is?' Kalf replied crossly, turning to glare at him.

Finn climbed up to the platform. He peered out, over the stockade, and saw that three armed men on horses were at the gate. One was close enough to bang on it with his fist, the other two were a little further back. They wore chain mail over leather tunics and had swords in scabbards on their belts. The pair at the rear wore round iron helmets but the man at the gate was bareheaded, his long, corn-yellow hair shining in the torchlight. He glanced up and Finn saw he had a moustache darker than his hair. His cheeks were smooth-shaven, and one side of his face was tattooed with a strange design of swirling lines. He grinned, showing teeth that had been filed to sharp points.

'Well then, what about you, boy?' he said. 'Are you going to let us in?'

Finn stared at him for a moment, not sure what to say. He hadn't expected the sea-wolves to arrive by land, if that's who they were. He hadn't expected to do any talking with a sea-wolf, either. And why were there only three of them? Surely there should have been more, a longship's crew. 'No, we're not,' he said eventually.

The man sighed and shook his head. 'That's not very friendly, is it, lads?' he said, and the pair behind him smiled. 'Still, no matter. I'm coming in anyway.'

He raised his legs, stood on his saddle and jumped, grabbing the top of the stockade and swinging himself over. He landed with a thump on the platform, his boots crashing down on the planks, his chain mail jingling. Finn and the others recoiled, startled by his sudden appearance. Finn tried to draw his sword but it stayed stuck in the scabbard. Ranulf threw his torch to one side and picked up his spear, which he had left propped against the stockade. He stepped forward, paused for an instant – then half-heartedly lunged at the man.

The intruder simply laughed and whipped out his sword, its blade flashing. He batted the spear away, knocking it out of Ranulf's hands, and immediately swung the sword back, chopping into Ranulf's neck. Ranulf looked startled, then sank to his knees and fell forward, blood spurting from a gaping slash in his throat.

Kalf gasped, stumbled backwards, and fell headlong off the platform. The man followed him, jumping down and landing on his feet again. Egil and Njal were there, and Finn watched helplessly as the man advanced on them, his sword held casually at his side. Ranulf's blood dripped off its edge and shone black in the torchlight. The man loomed over them, and it seemed as if Egil was about to raise his spear.

Finn froze, waiting for his friend to be cut down just like Ranulf.

That didn't happen. The man raised his sword, but shouted, 'BOO!' instead. Njal and Egil stumbled backwards like Kalf and fell over, then struggled to their feet and ran.

The man laughed more loudly, sheathed his sword, and turned to the gates. He lifted the cross-beam, throwing it aside as if it were a twig, and opened the gates wide. He brought in his horse, mounted, and trotted deeper into the village, glancing around, vanishing from sight for a moment down the main street before returning. He stopped below Finn on the platform and grinned up at him.

'Nice little village you have here,' he said. 'We'll be back.'

At last he kicked his horse forward and joined his companions outside the stockade. Finn watched them ride away, into the darkness from where they had come.

He felt as if his whole world had just collapsed around him.

CHAPTER SIX
Time to Die

A mass of villagers ran to the gates, mostly men and boys who had been on other parts of the stockade, but some women too. Bjarni was nowhere to be seen, and Finn remembered him running off. Kalf seemed to have survived, at least judging by the loud groans and curses coming from him. Finn went over to Ranulf, who lay in a pool of blood that was dripping through the walkway to the ground below.

'Is he dead?' said a trembling Njal, his voice hushed. Finn hadn't noticed until then that his friends had returned and climbed up the ladder to stand beside him.

'Of course he is,' said Egil. 'Nobody could survive a wound like that.'

One of Ranulf's eyes was still open, and in the torchlight the skin of his face seemed as white as fresh snow. But his throat was a dark mess of blood. Finn stared, unable to tear his eyes away, until his stomach twisted and foul-tasting bile filled his mouth. He turned and threw up, leaning far out over the top of the stockade. Njal and Egil rushed to help him, but he pushed them away.

'Don't touch me,' he snapped. 'I'm fine.' After a while he stood up straight and wiped his mouth on his sleeve. Then he took a deep breath and let it out slowly.

Suddenly, one of the women below them screamed, her voice cutting through the cold night air. 'It's Luta, Ranulf's wife,' said Njal, and they watched as the other women gathered round to hold her. But she refused to be comforted, and screamed even more loudly. Others began to arrive, among them Gunnhild's friend Signy, who burst into tears as well. Finn recalled that Ranulf was her grandfather.

'What shall we do, Finn?' Njal said eventually. 'You have to tell us.'

A chill wind came whispering down from the mountains, and the torch flames were blown sideways, flapping and flickering. Finn's mind was in turmoil, his heart pounding in his chest. He wanted to say that he had no idea what they should do, that he wished this nightmare was over – and that he wished most of all that his father had never left him in charge. But he had, and Finn knew he would have to deal with it.

'Close the gates,' he said. 'And bring Ranulf down for his wife.'

Finn looked out into the darkness, his eyes wet with tears.

* * *

In the morning Finn called another meeting. The villagers were scared and wanted to talk, but they went round in circles, asking the same questions and saying the same things over and over again. Solveig had recognised Kalf's description of the man with the tattoo and yellow hair, so there was no doubt he and his companions were the same sea-wolves who had attacked Andari's village. Somebody said they were probably a scouting party.

It seemed like a reasonable assumption. Solveig thought the horses could have been taken from her village, and Kalf said it was just the kind of thing that sea-wolves would do. The old man was unharmed from his fall, except for a few bruises. It certainly hadn't affected his ability to talk – but Finn stopped listening to him after a while, his mind returning to the blood spurting from Ranulf's throat, and the screaming of Ranulf's wife Luta when she had seen that her husband was dead.

Finn was no stranger to death. He was a farmer's son, so he had helped his father slaughter and butcher their animals, and he had wrung the necks of chickens and ducks. He had killed on the hunting trail, plunging his spear into rabbits flushed out of their warrens by dogs. He remembered the climax of a boar hunt last winter, when the beast turned at bay, killing two dogs before his father finished it off with his spear. Finn had even seen dead people before, those taken by age or illness.

But he had never seen a man killed with a sword. The most shocking thing had been the suddenness, the sheer speed of what had happened. Ranulf had been standing there, living and breathing, and then he had simply been cut down, his life's blood gushing from his throat. Leaping over the stockade, the killing – it had all been so easy for the tattooed sea-wolf, something he had clearly done many times before. And at that moment Finn realised just how crazy it was to think that a band of old men and young boys could hold off a whole crew of such deadly killers.

'Did you hear me, boy?' Kalf was saying, his grumpy, droning voice finally breaking into Finn's thoughts. 'I told you we should have fled into the forest while we had the chance to get away. It's still not too late, you know, even now.'

Finn looked at the old man on the other side of the hearth, and sighed. The same thought had occurred to him, but he had decided fleeing still wasn't the answer. 'Yes, I heard you, Kalf, and you're wrong. The man who killed Ranulf said they would be back, and they might already be close by, just waiting for night to fall. So if we left, we might walk straight into them, and that would be the end of us. No, it's better to stay here, inside the stockade. Then at least we have a chance to defend the village.'

'Is that so?' said a woman. 'You didn't do very well last night, did you?'

There was a swell of murmuring and Finn felt his cheeks burning. 'We will do better next time,' he said. 'They took us by surprise. That won't happen again.'

The woman didn't seem convinced, and Finn couldn't blame her. The meeting continued for a while longer. Many of the villagers seemed reluctant to go back to their houses, feeling happier perhaps to stay huddled together. But it broke up at last.

Finn watched the villagers shuffle out. He had already got Egil and Njal to round up the men and boys he had lost to their wives and mothers. There would no longer be two groups of guards. They would have to keep the walls manned day and night, no matter how tired they were. Now Finn sent Egil and Njal to make sure everyone was in position and staying alert.

He had set himself a special task, deciding that he really should go and see Ylva and Kjartan and get them to stay in the village while the danger lasted. So he left by the forest gate, making sure it was closed after him, and headed up the path to the forest, nervously looking around, half-convinced a sea-wolf lurked behind every tree. Ylva's hut was first, and Finn was relieved to see it was the same as ever, with puffs of grey rising from the roof's smoke-hole and Ylva outside, tending to her herb garden.

She looked round and put down her basket as he approached. 'The answer is no, Finn Ottarsson,' she said, fixing him with her gaze. He had never really noticed before how green her eyes were, nor how like the eyes of a younger woman.

'But... you don't know what I'm here to ask you,' Finn said, the small hairs prickling on the back of his neck as they often did when Ylva spoke.

'I do, and there is no magic to it,' she said with a smile. 'I know you have come to take me into the village. But I will be safe here. And if not, well then, I have had a long and good life, and perhaps the Fates have chosen this as my time to die.'

'Perhaps they have chosen it as the time for us all to die,' Finn said gloomily.

Ylva came closer to him, put a cool hand to his cheek and looked deep into his eyes. 'You are troubled, Finn,' she said. 'Tell me what is in your heart.'

Finn felt all the worries and doubts swelling inside him, and he knew that if he didn't let them out in some way he would burst. He had thought of speaking to Astrid, but he didn't want even her to know how terrified he was that he had made a huge mistake and was about to get everyone killed. Perhaps he could speak to Ylva...

The old woman listened, her head cocked to one side like a bird's, a faint smile on her lips until Finn fell silent at last.

'It is hard to carry such a burden alone, especially when you are so young,' said Ylva. 'You need the help of someone who understands the ways of warriors and can tell you what to do. Luckily for you, I know just the man.'

'It's too late, Ylva,' said Finn. 'I don't have time to send for anyone.'

'You don't have to,' she said, her smile broadening. 'The man I'm talking about is Kjartan. Come along now. We will go and pay him a little visit, you and I.'

Finn was surprised, and wanted to ask how an old man like Kjartan could know anything about warriors. But Ylva was already walking away from him, up the path, and moving quickly for a woman of her great age. Finn hurried after her, and they soon came to Kjartan's hut. It was much the same size as Ylva's, but closer to the trees, seeming almost to be sheltering under the thick arms of a great oak.

'Kjartan, show yourself!' said Ylva. 'There is a boy who needs your help.'

Nothing happened for a moment. Then the hut door creaked open and Kjartan stepped out. He stood in front of them and Finn realised that – unlike most of the old men in the village – Kjartan's spine was straight and his shoulders broad. He had a square jaw, and his eyes were the same blue as the icy sea in winter. He wore a clean brown tunic and trousers, and his long hair was tied back with a leather thong.

'Leave me alone, Ylva,' he said. 'I am too old and tired to help anybody.'

'Don't be ridiculous,' said Ylva. 'There's plenty of life in you yet. Besides, I'm sure you will want to help the boy when you know what danger he faces.'

'I doubt it,' said Kjartan, frowning. 'But I have a feeling you'll tell me anyway.'

'You're right,' said Ylva. 'A band of sea-wolves is coming to raid the village. Their leader is Red Swein, the man who killed your shield-brother Ingvar, father of Ottar the chief...' She paused to pull Finn forward. 'And grandfather of Finn here.'

Finn had been looking at Kjartan, but now he turned to Ylva, his mouth falling open with surprise. His mind raced as he tried to take in what she had said.

But there was more to come.

CHAPTER SEVEN
A Tool for Killing

The sky darkened suddenly, with a cold wind from the sea bringing sleet that stung the skin, and Kjartan invited Ylva and Finn into the warmth of his hut. Pine logs burned in the small hearth, snapping and crackling and filling the hut with the scent of the forest, but Finn barely noticed. He was too busy listening to Kjartan's tales of his early days as a Viking with Ingvar, the grandfather he had never known.

'Ingvar was my friend,' said Kjartan. 'I met him on my first Viking voyage. It was his first voyage too, and we were the two youngest in the crew. For us it was an adventure, a holiday from our boring lives at home, but all the others were hard men, interested only in plunder and slaves. Ingvar and I took care of each other, bench-mates at the oars, shield-brothers in battle. A bond like that doesn't break.'

'So does that mean you and my grandfather were... raiders?' said Finn. It was strange to think of this gruff old man as someone much younger, a warrior in his prime. It was stranger still to think of his own long-dead grandfather as a boy who had been bored by farming and wanted a different life, just like Finn himself. Perhaps it wasn't only the colour of your hair or eyes that you got from your family.

'If you're asking whether we were sea-wolves, then the answer is yes,' said Kjartan, turning to him. 'Oh, we did many things. We stole the gold from Christian churches and burned them down. We fought for lords and chiefs who paid us, and we switched sides when they ran out of money. And in between times we raided villages, running our keels on to beaches and leaping from our ships with fire and sword…'

Kjartan talked on, and for a short while it was as if the world Finn had glimpsed in old stories and legends filled the little hut. It seemed that Kjartan and Ingvar had travelled everywhere, and seen many wonders – and many terrible sights as well.

'Ingvar grew tired of it all eventually, and decided to settle down,' said Kjartan. 'He left the crew, went back to his village, married a pretty girl, had a fine son…'

'My father,' said Finn, and almost smiled to think of Ottar as a baby.

'But that isn't the end of Ingvar's story, is it, Kjartan?' Ylva said softly. 'Or yours, come to that. You must tell the boy everything, however painful it is for you.'

Kjartan turned to her now and held himself very still. Then he let out a great sigh, and his shoulders sagged. 'I missed my shield-brother, so I often came to visit him, and a few times I got him to come away with me for a summer's raiding. To be honest it was never that hard to persuade him, even though his wife hated the idea and didn't want him to go, fearing that he wouldn't return. And then one year... he didn't.'

Finn thought of his grandmother, this pretty girl who had lost her husband while she was still young. He had never met her, either – she had died a couple of summers before he was born. 'How did Ingvar die?' he said. 'Was it on a raid?'

'Yes, but we weren't doing the raiding,' said Kjartan. 'Our crew was being paid by a village to protect them from a new pack of sea-wolves led by a young Viking who was out to make his reputation. His name was Swein, and they called him Red Swein because he loved to kill, to make blood flow. He killed Ingvar, although it was a great fight and your grandfather left the mark of his blade-edge on Swein's face.'

'I... I think I found my grandfather's sword,' said Finn. 'It was in a chest in the storeroom, along with a helmet and a mail-shirt. They're very plain, though.'

'A sword is a tool for killing,' said Kjartan. 'Only kings and rich jarls have fancy weapons and armour. But then they're not the ones who do all the fighting.'

Finn fell silent for a moment, taking everything in. Then he remembered what he had heard a few days earlier about how life had been hard for his father after Ingvar had died. In one way, that had been Kjartan's fault – if Kjartan hadn't persuaded Ingvar to go with him, then he might have lived and things would have been easier for Ottar. 'Did you come here because you felt guilty, Kjartan?' Finn said.

The old man met his gaze, their eyes locking together. 'Partly,' he said eventually. 'But I was also old and tired and had nowhere else to go, and I wanted to see the son of my shield-brother before I died. You should be proud to have such a man as your father, Finn. He made me welcome in his hall because I had been his father's friend in our youth, and he has never blamed me for what happened.'

'Why didn't I know about all this?' said Finn. 'Why didn't he tell me?'

'Perhaps he didn't want you to think of your grandfather as a hero,' said Ylva. 'He knows what you boys are like, how you dream of Viking glory and fame.'

Finn felt the small hairs prickling on the back of his neck again. It was as if Ylva had been looking deep into his heart and could see everything it contained.

'There will be no glory or fame for me if Red Swein defeats us and destroys our village,' he said. 'But surely the Fates have brought him here for a reason.'

'I think you are right,' said Kjartan. He paused for the space of several heartbearts, as if he were thinking – and making a decision. 'And that is why I will help you,' he murmured at last. 'It is fitting for me to do what I can for the people of Ingvar and his son, and his grandson.'

'Forgive me for saying this,' said Finn. 'But what *can* you do for us? You said yourself that you are old and tired, and there is only one of you, and...'

Kjartan smiled, and it was like sea ice glittering in the midwinter sun.

'I can do more than you can imagine,' he said quietly.

And Finn found it easy to believe him.

* * *

Others found it harder. Finn quickly summoned the village to a meeting in his father's hall – perhaps the last they would ever have, if they failed, he thought with a pang. The people seemed even more frightened than before and came in grumbling and muttering. And when Finn said they were there to hear Kjartan speak to them about what they should do, many were very puzzled. Kalf was first on his feet to complain, of course.

'Kjartan? What nonsense is this?' he said. 'He's just a miserable old man.'

'It takes one to know one,' said Astrid. There was laughter, and some of the crowd jeered at Kalf. He went red in the face and started yelling, but suddenly the doors flew open and Kjartan strode in, the sky dark with rain clouds behind him. He was wrapped in a long black cloak and walked the length of the hall, his boots thudding on the rush-covered floor. Finally he stood beside Finn and faced everyone.

'Go back to your hut, Kjartan, we have no need of you!' said Kalf, sneering. 'I don't know what you've been telling the boy, but you can't fool me.'

'I swear by great Odin that he's not trying to fool you,' said Finn. 'Kjartan used to be a sea-wolf himself long ago, so he can tell us how to deal with them.'

Kalf gave a shout of laughter, then shook his head. 'A sea-wolf? Him? That's the most ridiculous thing I've heard in my life. I'd love to see him prove it...'

'Very well,' said Kjartan. He threw off his cloak to reveal he was now wearing a fine chain-mail byrnie that covered his body and arms and reached down to his knees. A thick belt of scarlet leather went round his waist, and a sword in a wooden scabbard hung down from it. Its grip was made of plain white ivory, the pommel was a small globe of yellow amber, and the hilt a simple curved piece of steel. A dagger in a sheath sat on Kjartan's other hip.

There were a few gasps from the crowd, as well as some murmuring. Finn thought everybody was probably thinking the same as him. Kjartan looked completely different – years younger, and a warrior from head to foot. Everybody except Kalf, that is. He crossed his arms and gave Kjartan a withering glare.

'I'm not convinced,' said Kalf. 'You'll have to do better than that.'

Kjartan didn't answer. Instead, he slowly drew his sword from its scabbard and held the blade out at his side. It glinted in the torchlight, and Finn could see the flames of the hearth-fire reflected in Kjartan's eyes, making him look like some creature of legend, a ghost-warrior perhaps, one who guards the tomb of an ancient king. Then Kjartan stepped towards Kalf and swung his blade in a tight arc, cleanly slicing the bushy tuft from the old man's head. The people on either side of Kalf leaped out of the way. A cloud of Kalf's white hairs drifted down to the floor.

'Satisfied?' growled Kjartan. 'Or do you want me to cut something else off?'

'No, I believe you,' squeaked Kalf, and swiftly sat back down on the bench.

'Well, I'm glad that's settled,' said Finn, trying not to look at Egil and Njal, who were both grinning. 'Perhaps we can get on to more important things now.'

'Tell me what has happened so far,' said Kjartan, re-sheathing his sword.

Finn did as the old Viking asked, explaining about the attack on Andari's village, the visit by the three sea-wolves the night before, the death of poor Ranulf. Others spoke too, particularly Solveig, who added details and answered Kjartan's questions. The hall fell into silence at last, and Kjartan stood in deep thought, his eyes narrowed.

'If Swein has gone north, it will take his scouts a while to find him,' he said. 'So it will be two days before he attacks, perhaps three. That gives us time to prepare.'

'We thought we were ready for them last night,' said Finn. 'But we weren't.'

'You came up with the best plan you could – seal the village, defend the stockade, keep them out,' said Kjartan. 'The trouble is, that's just what Swein will expect. And as you discovered, it didn't work against one man, let alone a whole crew.'

'It's our only hope though, isn't it?' said Finn. 'What else can we do?'

'We can give them a surprise,' said Kjartan with that icy smile of his. 'Instead of trying to keep them out, we will leave the gates open – and let them walk right in.'

There was even more murmuring now, and Kalf gave a squeak of protest. Kjartan turned to stare at him, and the old man seemed to shrivel under his gaze.

Finn, however, was struggling to understand what he had just heard.

CHAPTER EIGHT
Stolen Dreams

At first the idea of deliberately letting the sea-wolves into the village seemed utterly crazy, and people were confused. But Kjartan explained what he meant, and soon Finn – and everyone else in the hall – began to see how such a plan could work.

'Don't think of it as a battle, more as hunting a wild beast,' said Kjartan. 'What is the best way to kill a wild boar in the woods? He will rip you to pieces in a one-on-one fight. So, instead you lead him to a place where you can trap and surround him...'

'But it won't be just one wild beast, it will be a whole crew of them,' said Egil, and others murmured their agreement. 'How many sea-wolves can we expect, anyway?'

'Usually around thirty,' said Kjartan. 'Swein will probably leave a few men to guard his ship, then divide the rest into two groups, one entering by the forest gate, the other from the quayside. We will need to split them up even more, and make every dark spot somewhere to ambush them and cut down their number. That means we will need everybody in the village to be involved in the defence.'

'I hope we can count on *all* the men and boys this time...' said Finn, looking around. Several men avoided his gaze, as did some wives and mothers.

'That will not be enough,' said Kjartan. 'We need the women and girls too.'

There were even more gasps now, and several people called out angrily.

'Women can't fight warriors like the sea-wolves,' shouted an older man at the back.

'You told me there are fifty men and boys to defend the village,' said Kjartan. 'With that we will outnumber the sea-wolves by less than two to one. How many women and girls can we add to our band of hunters? Fifty or more? Then it would be at least three to one. Even a sea-wolf might baulk at those odds.'

'And don't forget, we women are fiercest when someone threatens our young,' said Astrid, her voice ringing out loud and clear. 'A she-wolf fighting to protect her cubs is a terrible thing to behold, and we have many cubs to protect in our village.'

'Some of those cubs can take care of themselves,' said Gunnhild. She was sitting beside her mother, but her eyes were defiantly fixed on Finn's. He returned her gaze and shrugged uncomfortably, unsure what to say. His father had told him to trust Astrid's judgement, and what she had said made sense. But Finn still had his doubts.

'Well, I suppose that's agreed then,' he said at last. 'What now, Kjartan?'

'I'll have a look round the village first,' said the old Viking. 'Then, once I've worked out how to set the traps, you farmers can do what you do best.'

'And what would that be?' said Finn, feeling puzzled.

'Digging,' said Kjartan with his wintry smile.

He strode out of the hall, and Finn followed.

* * *

It didn't take Kjartan long to work out his plan. He walked all over the village, Finn trailing in his wake with Egil and Njal, and finally climbed up to the stockade platform at the forest gate. Kjartan stood thinking for a moment, then nodded to himself.

'Yes, that will be the way to do it,' he murmured. 'Draw them into the heart...'

Kjartan was sure Swein would come at night, and said they should empty all the houses, with everyone who would not be fighting – the very old and the very young – taking shelter in Ottar's hall. The rest of the villagers would be organised into small war-bands, each made up of ten or so fighters, armed as well as possible. Their task would be to hide throughout the settlement, ready to strike when the moment came. No torches or lamps would be left burning, so the place would be in total darkness.

'There is a quarter-moon tomorrow night, and it will not be that much bigger the night after...' Kjartan murmured. 'The sea-wolves will bring torches, but it should be easy for everyone to stay conccaled from them, at least to begin with.'

'Then what do we do?' said Finn. 'We can't beat them just by hiding.'

'Trust me, Finn Ottarsson, we will not be hiding long,' said Kjartan. 'When they see the houses are empty, they will think that you have fled into the forest. Most of them will make for the hall, hoping to find any plunder that has been left.'

'And that's when we attack,' said Finn. 'Just when they think we've gone.'

'Exactly,' said Kjartan. 'You trip them and stab them with knives and spears. You tangle them in fishing nets dropped from roofs and beat them with clubs. You shoot them with arrows from the shadows. You make sure they fall into the hidden pits you will be digging, the ones you are going to fill with sharpened stakes. You set fire to their cloaks and their hair, and you make sure always to stay ahead of them...'

If everything went to plan, there would be a lot fewer sea-wolves by the time they made it to the hall, where those that hadn't been killed could be surrounded.

'Do you think they will ask for mercy?' said Finn. Kjartan shook his head.

'Not while Red Swein lives,' he said. 'He is their lord and master, and they are sworn to follow him wherever he might lead, even if it is to their deaths.'

'But he might already have been killed,' said Finn. 'What will they do then?'

'Oh, you will not catch such a warrior in a fishing net,' said Kjartan. 'I think the Fates have a different end in store for Red Swein. I will be waiting for him at your father's hall, and perhaps what happens there will change things for his men.'

He said no more, but Finn noticed how he frowned and gripped the hilt of his sword. There was no time to ask what was in his mind, though – they had far too much to do. Finn sent Egil and Njal to round up as many people as possible to dig pits and prepare other surprises for the sea-wolves, and he was pleased to see that nobody argued. The villagers worked for the rest of that day, and some even kept going through the night. By morning the village was full of hidden traps.

Then it was time to organise the war-bands, and almost nobody argued about that, either. Finn called everyone to the hall once more, and he and Kjartan decided who would fight together and in which part of the village they would wait. Of course Kalf made a fuss, loudly demanding that he be made leader of his war-band, until Kjartan quelled him with a look.

'I think we should just let him have what he wants,' Finn whispered. 'It will be easier that way – he won't stop complaining otherwise.'

Kjartan shrugged. 'So be it,' he said. 'Little things loom big in small minds.'

A group of girls was hanging back – Gunnhild and Freydis and Signy, and half a dozen friends of the same age. They were all wearing rough tunics and trousers, and had their long hair tied up in ponytails. Gunnhild stepped forward at last.

'We girls are going to fight together,' she said. 'I'm just letting you know.'

'Well, thanks for that,' said Finn. 'We boys will try not to get in your way.'

'Good,' Gunnhild snapped, and walked away, the others following her.

Finn watched her go, then realised that Kjartan was looking at her with his eyes narrowed. 'She is a brave girl, that one,' he said. 'I only hope she lives.'

Finn went cold all over. Of course there was a possibility that Gunnhild might be killed, along with many more of the villagers, even if they did manage to fight off the sea-wolves. It was a sickening thought, and suddenly he wished he hadn't been so horrible to her just now, or at any time in the past. But he could do nothing about it, and he pushed the thought from his mind. Then something else occurred to him.

'We would all have a much better chance of living if you taught us some of your war-craft, Kjartan,' he said. 'It would be a great honour to learn from you.'

'There is not that much to learn, Finn Ottarsson,' said Kjartan. 'You shouldn't believe what you hear in the songs and stories. True, there are a few great fighters, but it takes talent and years of experience to become one. Fighting is brutal and savage, and most Vikings are just killers, the kind of men who never think of glory and fame, and who will stab you in the back if it is the easiest way to win.'

'I... I didn't know...' Finn murmured, unable to hide his disappointment.

'Ah, so Ylva was right, you do want to be a Viking, and now I have crushed your dreams,' said Kjartan. 'I will tell you one thing, though. It is hard to stand in the shield-wall and fight against men who want to kill you. But it is much harder to be a farmer, to build a village and bring children into this world of woe and protect them. Your father is ten times braver, no, a hundred times braver than any Viking.'

Finn had no more questions for Kjartan after that.

* * *

They were ready for the sea-wolves that evening, but they didn't come. They didn't come the next day either, and time seemed to pass very slowly for Finn. He went round checking on everybody until Egil and Njal told him to stop, then he paced up and down in front of his father's hall, worrying. The hall itself was packed with the very young and very old, looked after by Astrid. Ylva had come to help her.

It had been cold all day, the sky a pale blue, and once the sun went down it grew even colder. The moon appeared, a curved sliver of silver, and soon frost glittered on every surface. Finn waited with Egil and Njal in the shadows by a house near the quayside gate, their breath making clouds in the chill air. The gate was open, the sea calm, almost sluggish, the moon's twin riding gently on its surface. The village was quiet except for the lowing of cattle and the bleating of sheep in their pens.

'I wish they'd hurry up,' Egil muttered, his teeth chattering. 'I'm frozen.'

'You'll soon warm up if they do come,' said Njal. 'Wait... what's that?'

Finn had seen something too, a dark shape moving on the water. He peered into the night, and realised it was a sleek longship making for the shore. Its sail was furled, both banks of oars were beating up and down like the wings of some great bird, and the only sound was a gentle splashing. A warrior stood by the dragon prow, his chain mail gleaming in the moonlight, with more men behind him. The longship hit the beach, its keel grinding on the sand, and the warrior leaped down, his sword drawn.

It seemed that Red Swein had arrived at last.

CHAPTER NINE
Two Blades

Finn sent Egil and Njal running off to tell everyone, then stepped further back into the shadows, making sure he couldn't be seen from the gate. He watched as a dozen or so sea-wolves entered the village, several of them holding flaming torches aloft. Red light glinted off the blades of their swords and axes and spears. They fanned out in a wide semi-circle facing the houses, and Red Swein walked in behind them.

He was just as Solveig had described him – the raven-black hair with a white stripe through it, the scar running over one eye. But Solveig hadn't mentioned the cruel mouth, or the air of evil and menace that seemed to crackle around him as he scanned the village, like some great eagle searching for its prey. He wore a billowing cloak that was the colour of blood, and he held his sword casually at his side.

'Well, this isn't much of a welcome, is it, lads?' he said with a wolfish grin. 'We'd better find out if the villagers are still at home, or whether they've run off.'

His men moved forward and kicked in the doors of the nearest houses. Finn slipped away, keeping to the shadows as he ran along the main street. He passed groups of fighters waiting in the shadows, and glimpsed more on the roofs. Eventually he came to the open space in front of his father's hall, where Kjartan stood waiting. Just at that moment Egil and Njal came running up from the other end of the village.

'It's as you thought, Kjartan,' said Egil. 'They're at the forest gate too.'

Suddenly a light blossomed in the darkness, as flames leaped from the roof of a house down by the quayside gate. Finn could hear the sea-wolves cheering.

'Time to unleash the hounds, boys,' Kjartan growled. 'Let the hunt begin!'

Finn grinned now too, and realised from the expressions on the faces of Egil and Njal that they felt the same mixture of terror and excitement as he did. He turned and ran back towards the quayside gate to get things going, his friends doing the same in other parts of the village. Two more houses had gone up in flames by the time Finn reached the first group of fighters, and they were impatient to get started. A sea-wolf was swaggering up the street towards them, unaware they were there.

Finn nodded, and a net came swirling down from a roof on to the sea-wolf, tangling him in its folds. The fighters – older men, with a few women – emerged from the shadows, but they hesitated, seemingly unsure about what to do next. Finn's heart sank – if they couldn't do what they had to, the plan wouldn't work. Then Solveig pushed through the others and rammed a spear into the sea-wolf's chest, penetrating the chain mail. 'That's for Andari,' she hissed, but the man was already dead.

The other fighters looked shocked, and Finn knew he had to say something. 'You see? They are not gods, and Solveig has shown you how easy it is to kill them!'

He ran on, hurrying to find the next group so he could encourage them as well. But there was no need – they had also made a kill, and soon Finn could hear yelling and screaming from elsewhere in the village. Kjartan's plan was working – three sea-wolves fell into hidden pits and were impaled on the stakes at the bottom, and Finn saw three more brought down and killed with spears or beaten with clubs.

It didn't all go the villagers' way – some of the sea-wolves fought them off, wounding half a dozen and killing two of the older men.

There was no time to grieve, though – Finn kept everyone pushing the sea-wolves to where they wanted them.

At last he returned to his father's hall. Kjartan was where Finn had left him, but now the villagers had formed a wide circle around the open space. Many held torches, their leaping flames bright against the darkness, the flickering light falling on the surviving sea-wolves. They stood back to back in the centre of the circle, their swords pointed at those surrounding them. Finn could see there were no more than fifteen or sixteen sea-wolves left, and several were bleeding from wounds.

'Kill them all!' screamed a woman in the crowd, and Finn realised it was Luta, Ranulf's widow. Her granddaughter Signy stood beside her, and so did the rest of the girls' war-band led by Gunnhild. Finn's heart leaped when he saw that his stepsister was still alive, and that her spear-blade – and those of her friends – were stained with blood. Gunnhild saw him looking at her and grinned, and Finn smiled back. Egil and

Njal had survived as well, and took their place beside him.

There was more yelling in the crowd, like a pack of hounds baying for blood. The sea-wolves yelled too, calling out curses and bloodthirsty threats.

'We cannot kill them all yet, because they are not all here,' said Kjartan, his voice booming out. Everyone instantly fell silent. 'Where... is... Red Swein?'

'I am here,' said Red Swein from behind the far side of the circle. He pushed through, roughly shoving several people out of his way. Another sea-wolf followed, and Finn realised it was the tattooed warrior who had killed Ranulf. Both walked forwards slowly, swords held at their sides, and neither seemed particularly worried. If anything, Swein seemed faintly amused. 'Wait, don't I know you?' he said, staring at Kjartan with narrowed eyes. 'By the gods, Eirik, look! It's Kjartan!'

'So it is,' said Eirik, the tattooed warrior. 'It must be twenty years since we saw him last. We fought him and his friend in that village... what was his name?'

'Ingvar,' growled Kjartan. 'And you killed him, Swein.'

'Ah yes, I remember him well,' said Swein, raising his left hand to touch the scar over his eye. 'And I'm guessing these farmers paid you to organise their defence against us, just as you did back then. Well, you've done a marvellous job.'

'Oh, I don't know, Swein,' said Eirik. 'We weren't expecting them to set traps for us, were we? It's one thing to dig pits for us to fall into and to sneak up on us in the dark. It's something else to face a crew of angry sea-wolves in the open...'

Eirik strode up to the nearest villagers and snarled at them. But even though they looked scared, they held their ground and several jabbed at him with spears. He batted the spears away with his sword, but he also quickly stepped back.

'They are not paying me, Swein,' said Kjartan. 'This is Ingvar's village, and the Fates have brought you here so I can take vengeance on you for his death.'

'And I am Ingvar's grandson,' said Finn, stepping forwards, gripping the hilt of his grandfather's sword. This time the blade seemed almost to leap from the scabbard.

'Is that so?' said Swein, his wolfish grin returning. 'Well, I don't have to worry about a mere boy, even one with a sword. But you might be a different matter, Kjartan. There was a time when you were known all across the North as a great fighter... what did they call you? Kjartan Skull-splitter? But now you are old, so perhaps the Fates have brought me here to send you to Valhalla instead...'

Suddenly Swein attacked, springing at Kjartan, swinging his sword in a sweeping arc at his head. Kjartan raised his sword to parry the blow, and the two blades crashed together with a clang. Swein struck at him again, and Kjartan parried the second blow, then swung his blade at Swein in turn. There were gasps and screams from the crowd, and the sea-wolves cheered, egging on their leader.

Finn watched, fascinated, as Swein and Kjartan fought their duel. It was clear they were both great fighters, the kind of whom Kjartan had spoken. They soon settled into a rhythm of blow and counter-blow, a duel that looked like a dance. Their blades flashed and flew, striking blue sparks off each other, and for a while Finn was sure that Kjartan would win. His blade moved more quickly, testing and probing, and Swein began to give ground, grunting with effort, his face pale and grim.

But Kjartan faltered at last, and Finn could see that the old Viking's chest was heaving, his breath coming in gasps. Swein stopped retreating, and laughed.

'I was right,' he said. 'You're good, Kjartan, but age has stolen your strength, and soon we will find out if it's true that an old man's blood is as thin as water.'

Then he swiftly strode forward, chopping and hacking at Kjartan, using his sword more like an axe to beat down his opponent. Now it was Kjartan's turn to give ground, and he moved slowly back towards the hall, trying to hold Swein off. Everyone was yelling, the sea-wolves for Swein, the villagers for Kjartan. Finn kept yelling, 'Kjartan! Kjartan!' over and over, desperately willing him to win.

It was not to be. Kjartan stumbled and fell backwards, dropping his weapon. Swein paused for a brief instant – and plunged his sword deep into Kjartan's chest. Then he yanked the blade free, raising it in triumph as his men shouted their approval.

Finn ran over to Kjartan and knelt beside him. Dark blood flowed from the old Viking's chest, and red bubbles had formed at the side of his mouth. He wasn't dead yet, though, and he gripped Finn's arm. 'Ingvar's... sword...' he whispered, his eyes glittering fiercely. 'Use... Ingvar's... sword.' Then the light in his eyes went out.

Finn eased Kjartan's hand from his arm and rose to his feet. Swein was facing away from him, taking the acclaim of his men. 'Are you ready for some fun, lads?' he was yelling. 'We're going to kill them all and burn this village to the ground!'

The villagers looked terrified, and some were already turning to flee. Suddenly Finn felt a cold fury rise from the pit of his stomach and flow into every part of him, from his toes to his fingertips. He felt as if he might almost burst.

'Red Swein!' he screamed, striding forward. Swein turned round, just in time for Finn to ram Ingvar's sword through his chain mail, into his gut and out through his back. The sea-wolf toppled over, his eyes wide with surprise.

A deep silence fell, and for an instant all that could be heard in the open space before Ottar Ingvarsson's hall was the sound of the torch flames flickering in the cold wind. Then the villagers roared, and swept over Red Swein's men like the sea.

Finn sank to his knees and felt the fury drain out of him.

The village was safe.

CHAPTER TEN

Viking Funeral

O ttar returned four days later, the two trading ships arriving at the quayside with the morning flood tide. Finn was there to meet his father and accompany him back to the hall. There, he told him everything that had happened since he had been away.

'We managed to stop the fires spreading,' Finn said at last. They were standing outside the hall, looking down on the village. 'So we only lost six houses.'

'Houses can be rebuilt,' said his father. 'But we can't bring back the dead. Not those who died here, nor those who died in poor Andari's village, for that matter.'

Another five people had died in the battle with the sea-wolves, three men and a woman, and young Bjarni, who had fought bravely. More had been wounded, and Astrid and Ylva were caring for them. Eight of the sea-wolves lived, though not Eirik, the tattooed warrior – Ranulf's widow Luta had made sure that he died. The rest had surrendered, and were being held captive in an animal shed, along with the three men Swein had left to guard his ship. A dozen people from Andari's village had also been on the ship. They had been taken to be sold as slaves, but they were free now.

'I know,' said Finn. 'I wish I could have done better, and saved them...'

'You did your best, Finn, and I am very proud of you. And I am sure that your grandfather would have felt the same. His Viking blood runs in your veins.'

'But I'm glad your blood runs in my veins too – the blood of a farmer. I wanted to ask you, Father – can I come with you on the trading voyage next year?'

'Of course you can!' Ottar smiled, and squeezed Finn's shoulder.

'Although I do have one condition...' Finn said, looking into his eyes.

'Oh yes?' said his father, his smile fading. 'And what would that be?'

'I want to give Kjartan a proper Viking funeral – in Swein's ship.'

'Do you, now?' Ottar frowned. 'You do realise we could sell that ship, don't you? It's a beautiful craft and we could get a pretty price for it.'

'I know that, Father. But we owe it to Kjartan to give him the best send-off we can on his journey to Valhalla. That's what I think the Fates always intended.'

'So be it,' said Ottar. 'It will be a fitting end to Kjartan's story.'

* * *

They spent the rest of the day preparing Kjartan and the ship for their last voyage. Astrid and Ylva had already cleaned the old Viking's body and combed his grey hair. Now they dressed him in his chain mail and a fine bearskin cloak that they had found in his clothes chest. Then Ottar and some of the men laid him on a wooden bier in the ship's central gangway, his head aligned with the dragon prow. And finally Finn bent the dead man's fingers around the hilt of Ingvar's sword.

All the villagers gathered on the quayside as the sun sank into the dark sea. Ottar had ordered that the captive sea-wolves should be brought to the quayside as well. Finn wondered what he intended to do to them. Egil was convinced that he was going to cut their throats as sacrifices to make Kjartan's journey easier. Judging by the looks on their faces as they arrived, the prisoners themselves thought they were doomed.

But Ottar ordered that they be freed. 'Enough blood has been shed,' he told them. 'Just leave before I change my mind.' The sea-wolves did as they were told, and hurried off back through the village.

Then it was time to bid farewell to Kjartan. Finn stood on the quayside with his father and Astrid and Gunnhild, with Egil and Njal nearby, all of them watching as the men in two small boats tied lines to the longship and slowly pulled it out to sea. Eventually the wind caught its sail, and the men threw torches into the piles of kindling that surrounded Kjartan on his bier, then cut the lines so they could row away. Soon flames were leaping high into the dark sky, and a red glow spread across the water like blood.

Such was the tale of Finn, son of Ottar, son of Ingvar.

And now his tale is done.

Historical Note

'Alba', where Finn's story is set, is the Gaelic name for Scotland. In the Viking Age – from the 8th to the 11th centuries – people from Norway founded settlements on the west coast of Scotland and in the islands of the Orkneys and the Hebrides. They called the Hebrides 'The Southern Isles', which was logical for them, as they came from the North.

There were chiefs and other important men among the people who founded such settlements, but unlike Ottar they didn't always get their own way. The great Icelandic 'Sagas' describe the way of life in these settlements, and they often mention meetings at which disputes were settled. There are also plenty of strong females in the sagas – the kind of women and girls, like Astrid and Gunnhild, who were always prepared to fight for their families.

Fire was an essential part of Viking funerals. It was said the god Odin had decreed that a Viking should be burned when he died, and his ashes cast into the sea.

Glossary

Alba	the Gaelic name for Scotland.
Byrnie	a shirt made of chain mail to protect a warrior in battle.
Freya	the most important Norse goddess.
Great Ocean	the Atlantic.
Knarr	a trading ship.
Longship	a ship used by warriors.
Odin	the main Norse god, leader of all the other gods.
Shield-brother	a fellow warrior who fights at your side.
Shield-maiden	another word for a Valkyrie (see below).

Shield-wall	a tactic used by the Vikings in battle. Warriors linked their shields together to form a defensive wall.
Stockade	a wall made of logs with sharpened points, built to surround and protect a village.
Thor	a very important Norse god whose weapon was a great hammer called Mjolnir.
Valhalla	a hall in Asgard, home of the Norse gods, where brave warriors went after they died in battle.
Valkyries	women warriors from Norse legends, sent by Odin to collect warriors who died in battle and bring them to Valhalla.
Vikings	Norse warriors, raiders and explorers.

**Look out for more historical fiction
from Tony Bradman...**

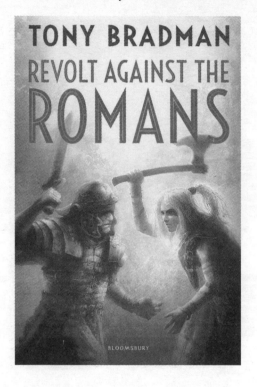

Young Roman Marcus is headed for Britannia,
an island at the end of the known world, and a
place where his destiny will change forever...

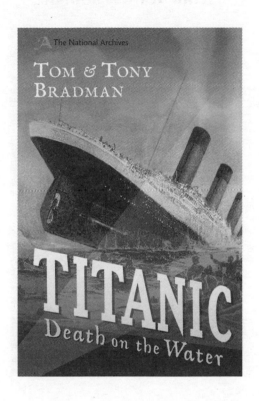

A Belfast boy is terrified of getting a job in the
dockyard where the Titanic is being built, and
where his father died. Instead he gets a job on
the ship, where he thinks his biggest problem is
his rivalry with a fellow ship's boy...

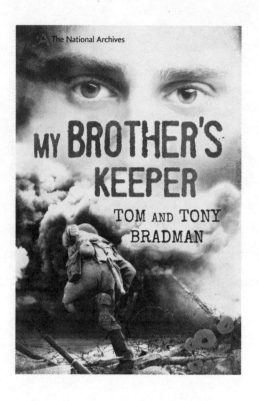

The Great War has begun. An underage boy
signs up for the Army to be like the other men
fighting for his country, but the reality of war is
very different from his dreams of glory...

For more great historical fiction from
Bloomsbury, visit www.bloomsbury.com